BREAKFAST AT TIFFANY'S

TRUMAN CAPOTE

LEVEL

RETOLD BY KIRSTY LOEHR

ILLUSTRATED BY TAYLOR DOLAN

SERIES EDITOR: SORREL PITTS

Contains adult content, which could include: sexual behavior or exploitation, misuse of alcohol, smoking, illegal drugs, violence and dangerous behavior. This book includes content that may be distressing to readers, including abusive or discriminatory treatment of individuals, groups, religions or communities.

PENGUIN BOOKS

UK | USA | Canada | Ireland | Australia
India | New Zealand | South Africa

Penguin Books is part of the Penguin Random House group of companies whose addresses can be found at global.penguinrandomhouse.com.
www.penguin.co.uk www.puffin.co.uk www.ladybird.co.uk

Penguin Readers edition of *Breakfast at Tiffany's* published by Penguin Books Ltd, 2022
002

Original text written by Truman Capote
Text for Penguin Readers edition adapted by Kirsty Loehr

Illustrated by Taylor Dolan

Printed and bound in Great Britain by Clays Ltd, Elcograf S.p.A.

The authorized representative in the EEA is Penguin Random House Ireland, Morrison Chambers, 32 Nassau Street, Dublin D02 YH68

A CIP catalogue record for this book is available from the British Library

ISBN: 978-0-241-54255-2

All correspondence to:
Penguin Books
Penguin Random House Children's
One Embassy Gardens, 8 Viaduct Gardens,
London SW11 7BW

Contents

People in the story

The writer

Holly Golightly

Joe Bell

Mag Wildwood

José Ybarra-Jaegar

New words

birdcage

brownstone

fire escape

guitar

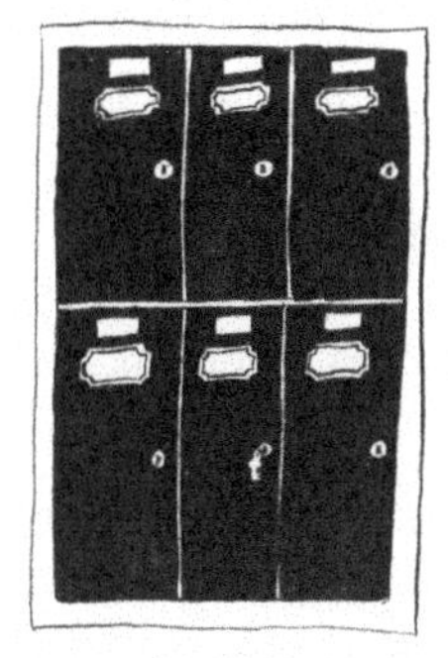

mailboxes

St. Christopher medal

Note about the story

Truman Capote (1924–1984) was an American writer. He first wrote short stories and then began writing longer books in 1948. Capote's most famous book, *Breakfast at Tiffany's*, was written in 1958. In the story, an unnamed writer remembers living in New York City in the United States of America during World War II. He becomes friends with one of his neighbors, the beautiful and strange Holly Golightly.

During the 1940s, women were not very **independent***. They usually got married and looked after their children while their husbands went to work. In *Breakfast at Tiffany's*, Holly is a different kind of woman. She is not married, she does not have children, and she has a lot of **independence**.

Breakfast at Tiffany's is a story about money, independence, and happiness. Holly wants to be independent, but she needs money (usually given to her by rich men) to help her live this way. When she is sad, Holly likes to stand outside Tiffany's, an expensive **diamond** store in New York City. For Holly, Tiffany's is her only "home" and the place where she **belongs**.

Before-reading questions

1 Look at the pictures in the book. What do you think the story will be about?

2 Read the "Note about the story." What is Tiffany's, and which city is it in? Have you ever been to this city?

*Definitions of words in **bold** can be found in the glossary on pages 78–80.

CHAPTER ONE
Holly Golightly, *traveling*

In the early 1940s, I lived in my first New York apartment in a brownstone in Manhattan. The apartment had one room and a window next to the fire escape. The walls were brown, and it had one bed, two chairs, and an old table. It was small and dark, but it was my first home and the best place for me to write.

Holly Golightly lived in the apartment below mine, and Joe Bell's bar was across the street. Holly and I went to Joe Bell's bar six or seven times a week to use his telephone. Holly got many messages, which Joe always wrote down for her.

Of course, this was many years ago, but last week, on Tuesday afternoon, the telephone rang. It was Joe Bell. Joe and I did not talk that much, but sometimes I went to the bar to see him. Joe was difficult to talk to. The only things he liked talking about were dogs, soccer, and Holly Golightly. I guessed that he was calling about Holly when he rang me.

"Can you come to the bar? It's important," he said.

When I arrived, I saw Joe. He was a small man with a strange face. His hair was thick and white, and his face was always red. Now it looked even redder. The bar was quiet and looked the same as it did all those years ago. There were two old mirrors on the wall and soccer photographs behind the bar. It did not have a television or any bright lights, and there was always a bowl of flowers that Joe chose himself.

"Something strange has happened," Joe said when he saw me.

"Have you heard from Holly?" I replied.

"Do you remember Mr. I. Y. Yunioshi?" he said.

"Yes, he had an apartment above me when I lived in the brownstone. He was a photographer," I said.

"I saw him last night for the first time in two years," he replied. "Do you know where he's been?"

"Africa?" I said.

Joe looked surprised. "How did you know?"

"I read it in a newspaper," I said.

He picked up three photographs and gave them to me. "Did you read *this* in a newspaper?"

The photographs all showed the same thing. There was a tall African man wearing a colorful skirt. He was smiling and holding a **carving** of a woman's head that was made from wood. The carving had large eyes and short hair. Her mouth was wide and smiled like a **clown's**. It looked just like Holly Golightly. I turned one of the photographs over and saw the words *African Carving, Tococul, Africa 1956.*

"What do you think of that?" Joe said.

"Well, it looks like her," I replied.

"Listen!" he said, hitting his hand on the bar angrily. "It *is* her, and Mr. Yunioshi agrees with me!"

"Did Mr. Yunioshi see her in Africa?" I asked.

"No, but Holly visited the African man's village with two

men. The men became ill, so they stayed in the village for a few days," Joe said. His face was even redder than before.

"And then?" I said.

"The two men and Holly left. Mr. Yunioshi looked for her, but he never found her," Joe said.

I looked at the photographs.

"She has probably never been to Africa," I said, but I could see her there, and it was somewhere she might go.

"Well, if you know so much, where is she?" Joe shouted.

"She's dead, or in prison, or married," I replied. "Yes, I think that she is married and living in Manhattan."

Joe was silent for a moment. "No," he said, shaking his head. "I've walked around Manhattan looking for her many times, and I've never seen her. Sometimes I see women who look like her. A thin girl who walks fast and straight, with a flat little bottom."

He was silent for a moment.

"I didn't know that you were in love with her," I said.

Joe's face was now pink. He picked up the photographs and stopped talking. Two men came into the bar, and it seemed the right time to leave, so I walked toward the door.

"Wait," Joe said, touching my arm. "Do you really think it's not her?"

"It doesn't matter, Joe," I replied. "She's gone."

"Yes," he said, opening the door. "She's gone."

When I got outside, I walked across the street toward the brownstone. The street had many large trees that looked beautiful in the summer. But today it was cold, and the leaves were yellow. The brownstone was next to a church with a blue clock that rang every hour. The brownstone looked different now, and the doors and windows were not the same. There was only one person I knew who still lived there. Her name was Madame Sapphia Spanella, and every afternoon she went skating in Central Park. I knew she was still there because I saw her name on the mailbox. It was one of these mailboxes that first introduced me to Holly Golightly.

One week after I moved into the brownstone, I noticed the words, "Miss Holiday Golightly, *traveling*" on a card on the mailbox of apartment two. The words interested me, and I could not stop thinking about them. A few days later, in the middle of the night, I woke up to hear Mr. Yunioshi shouting on the stairs. "Miss Golightly!" he said. "Stop ringing my doorbell, you must take a key!"

"Oh, I'm sorry. I always lose them!" a young and excited voice shouted back.

"I have to go to work in the morning, and I need to sleep!" Mr. Yunioshi replied, angrily.

"Oh, don't be angry, you sweet little man. I won't do it again, I promise!" the voice said.

I opened my door and looked down the stairs. I could see Holly, but she could not see me. She was wearing a black dress, black shoes, and an expensive pearl necklace round her neck. She had short blond-and-brown hair, and her mouth was wide like a clown's. She was followed by a short, fat man in an expensive suit. He was touching her arm.

"Thank you for walking me home," she said, closing the door in his face.

"I thought you liked me!" the man shouted, angrily knocking on her door.

Holly did not ring Mr. Yunioshi's doorbell again because the next day she started ringing mine. We never spoke, but every time I saw her late at night, she was wearing dark glasses and expensive clothes. Once, I saw her in a restaurant. She was sitting at a table with four men who were all smiling at her while she looked bored. Another time, it was in the middle of summer and too hot to stay inside. I went for a walk, and at the end of the street was a store with an old, large birdcage in the window. I wanted to buy the birdcage, but it cost $350, which was too expensive for a poor writer. On my way home, I saw a group of soldiers singing and dancing with a girl. It was Holly Golightly. The soldiers looked happy. They sang while Holly danced in their arms.

During that summer, Holly kept ringing my doorbell after midnight. Still, we never spoke, but I learned a lot about her. I knew what little food she ate because I looked in her **trash**. I knew what newspapers she read because I saw them outside her door. I knew that she smoked special cigarettes called Picayunes and that she had a red cat. I also knew that she played the guitar because, on sunny mornings, she sometimes sat on the fire escape with it. She played very well, and sometimes she sang. Her voice was interesting and beautiful.

Then one day, as the summer changed to fall, we finally spoke.

CHAPTER TWO
The weather report

I was at home having a drink when I had a feeling that somebody was watching me. Two seconds later, I heard a noise. It frightened me, and my drink fell on the floor. It was Holly, and she was standing on the fire escape, knocking on my window.

I got up and opened it.

"I've got the most horrible man downstairs," she said, while stepping off the fire escape and into my apartment. "He's sweet when he doesn't drink, but, when he drinks, he's horrible. If there is one thing I hate, it is men who bite."

She was wearing a gray robe. Her shoulder had a purple ring on it, so I could see what she meant by men who bite. The robe was all that she was wearing. My heart was moving so fast from the surprise of seeing Holly on my fire escape that it took me a moment to say anything.

"I'm sorry if I frightened you," she said. "He thinks I'm still in the bathroom, not that I care what he thinks. He'll get tired soon and go to sleep. I can leave if you want me to. But the fire escape was so cold, and you looked so warm inside, just like my brother, Fred. He was the only one in my family who allowed me to **hug** him on a cold night. Can I call you Fred?"

Holly stopped talking. She wasn't wearing her normal

dark glasses, and her eyes were large. They were a little blue, a little green, and a little brown. I didn't know her age, but she looked between 16 and 30. Later, I learned that she was 19.

"Do you think I'm wild?" she said.

"No, not at all," I replied.

She seemed **disappointed** with my answer. "Yes, you do. Everyone does. I like it—it's useful."

Holly moved her eyes across my apartment. "What do you do here all day?"

"I write things," I said, pointing to a table with books and paper.

"I thought most writers were old. Are you a real writer?" she said.

"What do you mean?" I replied.

"Well, do people buy what you write?"

"Not yet."

"I'm going to help you," she said. "I'm going to help you because you look like my brother, Fred, but he was much taller than you. It was the chocolate that made him tall. All he cared about was chocolate and horses. I haven't seen him since I was fourteen—that's when I left home. Poor Fred. I hope he can get chocolate now that he's a soldier."

"Why did you leave home so young?"

She touched her nose uncomfortably. "Tell me about something that you've written," she said, changing the conversation.

"That's the problem," I said. "My stories are not stories that you can *tell*."

"OK. Get me a drink, and then you can *read* me a story."

I made her a drink and sat in the chair opposite her. While I was reading, I suddenly became worried. It was a new story about two women who worked as schoolteachers and lived in the same house. One of the women decides to get married, but the other woman becomes jealous and tries to stop it. When I finished reading, I could see that Holly was bored.

"Is that the end of the story?" she asked, trying to think of something else to say. "Of course, I like **lesbians**, but this story is boring."

"What do you mean?" I said, angrily. "It's not about lesbians."

"Well, if it's not about two lesbians, then what is it about? I lived with a lesbian in Hollywood. She was better to live with than any man. Of course, everyone thought I was a lesbian, too, but who cares? Do you know any lesbians? I'm looking for someone to live with me."

Suddenly, Holly looked at the clock on the table. "It's 4 A.M.! What day is it today?"

"Thursday," I said.

"Oh no, I don't have time to sleep. I must stay awake."

"Why? What happens on a Thursday?" I said.

"On Thursdays, I have to catch the 8:45 train to Sing Sing prison. He prefers that I visit him in the morning."

"Who?" I asked.

"You have to promise me that you won't tell anyone," she said. "His name is Sally Tomato, he's a lovely old man, and he likes me very much. Maybe you have read about him?"

"No," I said.

"Well, I visit him every Thursday. We talk for about an hour, and then his lawyer, Mr. O'Shaughnessy, pays me $100."

"Why?"

"Mr. O'Shaughnessy called me on the telephone not long after Sally went to prison. He wanted me to visit Sally because he was all alone. I knew that Sally was in the **mafia**, but I didn't mind." Holly looked at me and smiled.

"Do you think that I'm lying?"

"No, but they can't allow anybody to visit a prison, can they?"

"I **pretend** to be his niece."

"So, you get $100 for just one hour of conversation?"

"Yes, as soon as I leave the weather report with Mr. O'Shaughnessy," she said.

"What is the weather report?" I asked.

"I tell him when there is a storm in Florida or when it's raining in Texas. Things like that."

"I think that you could get into a lot of trouble," I said.

"Don't worry. I have taken care of myself for a long time. I think you should go to sleep. It's late," she said, walking toward my bed. I followed her and got in.

"Don't say another word, and go to sleep," she said, getting in next to me.

We lay there quietly for a long time, and I pretended to sleep.

"Poor Fred," she said, suddenly. It seemed like she was talking to me, but she was not. "Where are you, Fred? It's cold, and there is snow in the wind."

I looked round at her face and saw that her eyes were wet. "Why are you crying?" I said. She sat up then walked toward the window and climbed on to the fire escape. "I hate people who ask too many questions," she said, angrily.

CHAPTER THREE
The party

The next day, I came home and found a message from Holly in my mailbox. *Thank you, Fred. You were so nice last night. I won't do it again.* I replied, *Please do*, and put it in her mailbox along with some cheap flowers. But she kept her promise, and I did not see or hear from her for many days, which **disappointed** me.

When Wednesday arrived, all I could think about was Holly, Sing Sing prison, and Sally Tomato. I wrote her a second message, *Tomorrow is Thursday*, and put it in her mailbox. The next morning, I found another message from Holly. *Thank you for helping me to remember. Can you come to my apartment for a drink tonight around 6 P.M.?*

I waited until ten minutes past six before knocking on Holly's door. A strange man answered. His bald head was small, his body was large, and gray hair grew from his nose. He was smoking a cigarette.

"Holly is in the shower," he said, shaking my hand. "Come in."

Holly's apartment was different from my own. There was nothing to sit on, and there were suitcases for tables. A large bookcase, a lamp, a bowl of yellow flowers, and Holly's red cat were the only other things in the room. I liked it very much.

"Did she invite you?" the man said.

I nodded.

"A lot of people come here, and they are not invited," he said, coldly. "How long have you known Holly?"

"Not long. I live upstairs," I said. He seemed happy with my answer.

"Is your apartment the same size?" he asked.

"No, mine is much smaller," I replied.

"This apartment is horrible. I don't know why Holly lives here," he said. "What do you think?"

"About what?" I said.

"Do you think she's a **phony**?"

"No, not at all."

"You're wrong. She is a phony, but she's also not. She believes all these things that she believes. I've tried so hard to help her, but she always says no. I like her, everyone likes her, but a lot of people don't like her," he said.

I did not know what to say, so I nodded my head again.

"I'm O. J. Berman," he said, pointing his cigarette at himself. "I'm a Hollywood movie **agent**. I met Holly a couple of years ago in California. She had big, thick glasses and a terrible **accent**. Nobody knows where she comes from because she lies so much. I wanted her to be an **actress**, so I helped her change her accent, and I taught her some French. Some people in Hollywood were interested, and she got an **audition** for a big movie. Then, one day, my phone rings. It's Holly, and she's gone to New York. I say, 'What are you doing in New York? You have a big audition tomorrow.' She says, 'I'm in New York because I've never been to New York.' She didn't come back, she missed the audition, and now she's here in New York. Maybe she will marry Rusty Trawler, too, because she wants to."

He stopped talking and waited for me to speak.

"Sorry, I don't know him," I said, finally.

"You don't know Rusty Trawler?" he said, surprised. "You can't know much about her if you don't know Rusty Trawler." He made a smoke ring with his cigarette and smiled.

"What lies are you telling him, O. J.?" Holly said, coming into the room. She was wearing the same gray robe that she wore a few days ago in my apartment. Her hair was wet from the shower and water was falling on the floor.

"I'm telling him that you're a difficult person," O. J. said.

"Fred knows that already," she replied.

"But you don't know that," O. J. said, still smoking his cigarette.

The red cat ran toward Holly. She picked it up and hugged it closely. The cat did not try to move and seemed happy in her arms.

"O. J. is horrible, but he knows a lot of important people in Hollywood," she said, taking the cigarette from O. J.'s hand. "O. J., can you help Fred? He's a writer."

"What do you want me to do?" O. J. said.

"I want you to help Fred and tell everyone in Hollywood what a wonderful writer he is," she replied. "You can help him sell his stories, and then he will be rich."

"I'll think about it," O. J. said.

"Don't forget me when you're famous, Fred," she said, walking back toward the bathroom. "And if anyone knocks on the door, invite them in."

CHAPTER FOUR
The mean reds

It did not take long for more people to arrive at the party. Some of them were soldiers, but most were much older men. I was left alone by the bookcase. More than half of the books were about horses while the others were about baseball, two topics that did not interest me. I picked up a book and pretended to read while studying Holly's guests at the same time.

There was one man who looked like an adult child. But it was the way he **behaved** that I noticed. He was busily making drinks, introducing himself, and choosing what music to play. It was Holly who was telling him to do it, *Rusty, can you make this? Rusty, can you do this, please?*

The man's name was Rutherfurd "Rusty" Trawler. In 1908, when Rusty was five years old, his parents died. They left him a lot of money, so Rusty became rich and famous. He had three **ex**-wives, and his life was always written about in the newspapers. I was not told these things. I read them in *The Baseball Report,* another book from Holly's bookcase. The book had newspaper stories between its pages of Rusty and his life. Some of them were about Holly and Rusty and their plans to get married.

"Are you enjoying reading about me, or do you like baseball?" Holly said, appearing behind me. She was wearing her dark glasses.

"What was this week's weather report?" I replied.

She did not look happy with my question.

"I like horses, but I hate baseball," she said, looking at the book in my hand. "I hate the sound of it on the radio, but I listen to it for homework."

"What do you mean?" I said.

"There are only a few things that men can talk about. If a man doesn't like baseball, then he must like horses. If he doesn't like either of them, well, he doesn't like girls."

I did not say anything.

"Have you spoken to O. J.?" she said.

"No."

"You should speak to him—it's a good idea, believe me."

"I do believe you, but I don't think that I have much to show him," I said.

"Go and talk to him. He can really help you."

"Like he helped with your audition?"

"He told you about that?" she said. "Yes, I should feel bad. Not because I wanted the job, but because I allowed him to dream. I was just using him. I could never be a Hollywood actress. It's too difficult. If you're intelligent, it's too **embarrassing**. I would like to be rich and famous. But I want to still be me, wake up in the morning, and have breakfast at Tiffany's. Do you need a drink?" she said, noticing my empty hand. "Rusty! Will you bring my friend a drink?"

Holly picked up the red cat from the floor. "Poor cat," she said. "Poor cat without a name. I know it's horrible that he doesn't have a name, but I can't give him a name. He will have to wait until he **belongs** to somebody."

"Doesn't he belong to you?" I said.

"No, we met next to the river one day. He is **independent** like me. I do not want to own anything. Not until I know that I've found the place where me and my things belong together."

"Where is that?" I said.

"I'm not sure. But I know what it's like." She smiled and put the cat back on the floor. "It's like Tiffany's. It's not because of the **diamonds**. I don't care about diamonds. Diamonds only look good on older women."

"So why do you like Tiffany's?" I asked.

"Do you ever have those days when you get the mean reds?" she said.

"Do you mean the blues?"

"No," she said, slowly. "The blues are when you're getting fat, or when the weather is bad. You are just sad. The mean reds are horrible. You're afraid, but you don't know what you're afraid of. You think that something bad will happen, but you don't know what. Have you ever had that feeling?"

"Yes, like when you are worried?" I said.

"OK, when you are *worried*. But what do you do about it?" she asked.

"A drink can help," I said.

"I've tried that, but it doesn't work," she said. "I usually get into a taxi and go to Tiffany's. It's quiet there, and nothing bad could ever happen at Tiffany's. When I find a nice place like Tiffany's, then I will buy some chairs and tables and give the cat a name."

I smiled.

"I was thinking about moving to Mexico with my brother, Fred, after the war," she went on. "Maybe buy a house next to the sea. I went to Mexico once. It's a wonderful country with many horses. Fred is good with horses."

Rusty Trawler appeared carrying my drink.

"I'm hungry," Rusty said, sounding like a child.

"Yes, Rusty, we won't be long," Holly replied.

"I want to go," he said.

"I want you to behave," Holly said, quietly. She sounded like his mother.

"You don't love me," Rusty said.

"Nobody loves people who are naughty," Holly said. "Go back to the guests, Rusty, and, when I'm ready to eat, we will go to a restaurant."

Rusty seemed happy with Holly's answer and walked away.

"You didn't answer his question," I said. "Do you love him?"

"You can make yourself love anybody," Holly said. "Anyway, he had a horrible **childhood**."

"Is that why he *behaves* like a child?"

"Rusty feels safer when he is behaving like a child," she said.

"And are you going to marry him?" I asked.

"I'm not even pretending I don't know he's rich," she said. "Houses in Mexico still cost money."

"*Traveling?*"

"The card on my mailbox?" she said. "Do you think that it's funny?"

"Not funny, just interesting," I replied.

"I don't know where I will be tomorrow, so I told them to write 'traveling' on the card. They are from Tiffany's. I didn't need those cards, but I felt like I **owed** them something because I spend so much time there. Now, are you going to make friends with O. J.?"

Before we could find O. J., we were interrupted by a very tall young woman who was standing at the door.

"H-H-Holly," she said, while waving her finger. "Why have you been h-h-hiding all these m-m-men?"

The woman was over six feet tall and taller than most of the men at the party. She spoke with a **stutter**.

"What are *you* doing here?" Holly said.

"Why, n-n-nothing, darling. I was upstairs working with Mr. Yunioshi. You sound angry, Holly. Are you b-b-boys angry at me for interrupting your p-p-party?" she said, while looking at the men in the apartment.

"Do you want a drink?" Rusty Trawler said.

"Yes, please," the woman said, touching his arm.

"There aren't any drinks," Holly said.

"Don't worry, Holly," she said. "I will just introduce myself to your friends."

She walked toward O. J. Berman who now looked even shorter.

"I'm Mag W-w-wildwood from Wild-w-w-wood, Arkansas."

Before Berman could introduce himself, one of the soldiers appeared and asked Mag Wildwood for her telephone number. In seconds, another man asked her to dinner. She was not beautiful like Holly, but I noticed her. And her stutter, made her more interesting.

"Who can tell me w-w-where the b-b-bathroom is?" she said.

"I can," Berman said, quickly, giving her his arm.

"That won't be necessary," Holly said. "She's been here before. She knows where it is."

As soon as Mag left the room, Holly turned to her guests and started to speak.

"It's really sad," she said, loudly. "You would think that it would show more. But she doesn't *look* ill. She looks fine. Don't you think she looks fine?"

The room was silent. The soldier who was holding Mag Wildwood's drink immediately put it down.

"She's been ill for a while . . ." Holly continued.

When Mag came back from the bathroom, everybody was quiet. Nobody wanted to talk to her any more, which made her angry. She began drinking more and shouting at Holly. She started an **argument** with a 50-year-old man and then fell to the floor.

"Get up," Holly said, putting on her jacket. The guests were waiting at the door. They were ready to leave, but Mag did not move.

"Fred, darling, can you put her in a taxi?" Holly said. "She lives at the Winslow. You're the best, Fred, thank you."

Suddenly, the guests were gone, and I was alone with a woman on the floor who was now sleeping. She was too tall for me to carry into a taxi, so I put a **pillow** under her head and left her to sleep.

CHAPTER FIVE
A sunny morning

The next day, I saw Holly on the stairs.

"You!" she said, running past me. "You left her on the floor in my cold apartment, and now she's awake with the mean reds."

I understood that Mag Wildwood was still in Holly's apartment. I was **confused** because last night she and Holly did not seem like friends.

Over the weekend, things became even more **confusing**. First, a South American man knocked on my door by mistake. He was looking for Mag Wildwood, so I told him to knock at Holly's apartment downstairs. He had brown hair and was wearing a nice suit. He was very handsome. Then, later that night, I saw him again outside the brownstone. He arrived in a taxi and was carrying many suitcases.

I stayed confused until the next day. It was Sunday, the sun was strong, and my window was open. I could hear voices on the fire escape. It was Holly and Mag. Holly was painting her toenails and Mag was knitting a sweater. Holly's red cat was sitting between them.

"I think you're l-l-lucky that Rusty is North American," Mag said.

"That doesn't mean anything," Holly replied.

"Darling, there is a w-w-war on at the moment."

"And, when the war is finished, I am leaving," said Holly.

"I don't feel that way. I l-l-love my country," said Mag. "The men in my family were great soldiers."

"Fred is a soldier," said Holly. "I don't know if he is a *great* soldier. I think the more stupid you are then the braver you are. He's pretty stupid."

"Fred?" Mag said, confused. "The boy upstairs? I didn't know that he was a soldier. But he does look stupid."

"He's not stupid. He just looks stupid because he's alone and he doesn't want to be. Anyway, he's a different Fred. I meant my brother, Fred."

"Are you calling your own b-b-brother stupid?" Mag said.

"If he's stupid, then he's stupid," Holly replied.

"You shouldn't say that about your brother. He is fighting for you, for me, and for all of us, in the war."

"OK, OK," Holly said.

"I like to laugh about things, but I am also a s-s-**serious** person, and I love my country. That's why I am sad about José." Mag stopped knitting for a moment. "Do you think he's handsome?" she said.

"Hmm."

"I just don't know if I can m-m-marry a Brazilian and then become a B-B-Brazilian. I don't know the language, and it's six thousand miles away."

"Why don't you learn the language?" Holly said.

"Nobody is going to teach P-P-Portuguese in New York City. The only thing I can do is try to make José forget about becoming the p-p-**president** of Brazil. Then, I can get him to move here."

Mag was silent for a moment, then she said, "I'm in love. You saw us together. Do you think I'm in love?"

"Does José bite?" Holly asked.

"Bite?"

"Does he bite you in bed?"

"No? Why? *Should* he?" Mag thought for a second. "But he does laugh," she said.

"That's good. I like a man who can laugh in bed," Holly said while looking at her toes.

"Yes, maybe," Mag said. She sounded unsure.

"OK. So he doesn't bite, but he laughs. What else does he do?"

Mag was quiet.

"Did you hear me?" Holly said.

"I heard you. It's not that I don't want to tell you, but it's so difficult to remember. I d-d-don't think about these things the way you do. They go out of my head like a dream. I'm sure that's normal."

"It might be normal, darling, but I don't like being normal," Holly said. "Listen. If you can't remember, why don't you try leaving the lights on?"

"Oh no, Holly. I can't leave the lights on."

"Who cares? What is wrong with leaving the lights on? Men are beautiful. José is beautiful. I'd say he was getting a cold plate of food."

"Shh. You are talking too loud," Mag said.

"You can't be in love with him then. Does that answer your question?"

"No. Because I'm not a cold person. I'm a warm person," Mag said. She was starting to sound worried.

"OK. Maybe you are a warm person. But if you don't want to look at him then maybe José feels very cold next to you."

"No, he doesn't. And you are wrong. I am in love with him," Mag said. "Did you know that it is always warm in Brazil? I don't know why I keep knitting him sweaters."

"Is there no winter?" Holly said. She sounded tired.

"It rains. It is warm, but it rains."

"Rain and warm weather. Actually, I'd like that," Holly said, **yawning**.

"Maybe you should go to Brazil and not me," Mag said.

"Yes," Holly said, lying down. "Maybe I should."

CHAPTER SIX
The argument

On Monday, I went to get my mail. On Holly's mailbox, there was a new name. *Miss Golightly* and *Miss Wildwood* were now traveling together. There was also a letter in my own mailbox. The letter was from a small university that wanted to **publish** one of my stories. The university could not pay me for the story, but I was still very happy. I ran upstairs to Holly's apartment and knocked on her door.

When she opened the door, I was too excited to speak, so I put the letter in her hand.

"They should be paying you," she said, yawning.

Then, she looked at my face, and she could see that I was happy and that I did not want advice.

"It's wonderful. Come in," she said, quickly changing her **yawn** into a smile. "I'll change my clothes, and I'll take you to lunch."

Holly's bedroom was the same as her living room. There were many suitcases on the floor and the only thing to sit on was a large double bed.

"I'm sure you know that Mag Wildwood has moved in?" she said. "She's quite stupid, so it's very useful. She loves to clean."

I could see that Holly was not very tidy. There were clothes all over the bedroom.

"Did you know that she's an actress?" Holly said, while

looking for something under the bed. "It's a good thing because she won't be in the apartment much. She's also getting married. He's a nice man, but he's a lot smaller than her."

She found a pair of green shoes from under the bed and put them on.

"Listen," she said. "I'm happy, I really am."

It was a beautiful day on that Monday morning in October 1943. To start, we had drinks at Joe Bell's bar then lunch in Central Park. We did not walk past the zoo because Holly said she did not want to see anything in a cage. We spoke about our childhoods. Holly spoke about swimming in the summer and Christmas trees and parties. Her childhood sounded very happy, which confused me.

"But didn't you leave home when you were very young?" I asked.

"My childhood wasn't nice, but yours sounded worse. I didn't want to make you feel bad," she said. "Anyway, I have just remembered that I should send some chocolate to Fred."

The rest of the afternoon was spent looking for chocolate as it was sometimes difficult to find during the war. Soon, I **realized** that we were near the store with the large birdcage, so I took Holly to see it. She could understand why I liked it, but, for her, it was still just a cage.

On our way home, we passed a clothes store.

"Let's steal something," Holly said, taking my arm and pulling me into the store.

Inside, it suddenly felt like everybody was watching me.

"Come on," Holly said. "Don't be scared."

The saleswoman was busy with a group of people who were trying on clothes. Holly picked up a hat and put it on her head. She chose another hat and put it on my head. She then took my hand, and we walked out of the store. It was as easy as that. We ran all the way home still wearing the hats.

"Have you stolen before?" I said.

"Yes, when I needed to," Holly replied.

After that, Holly and I saw each other often, until I found a job. There is not much to say about this job as it was boring. I worked from 9 A.M. to 5 P.M. most days, which made it difficult for me to see Holly. I sometimes saw her early on Thursdays, when she went to Sing Sing prison, and sometimes when she went horseback riding in the park. But most of the time Holly was sleeping when I came home from work. Sometimes, I had coffee with her when she woke up and got ready for the evening. She was always on her way out, but it was not always with Rusty Trawler.

When it was with Rusty Trawler, they were usually joined by Mag Wildwood and the handsome Brazilian José Ybarra-Jaegar. He seemed too intelligent to be in their group. He seemed important, which he was because his job sent him to Washington two or three days a week. I did not understand how he could talk and listen to Mag Wildwood and look at Rusty's stupid baby face.

A few months later, I was waiting for a bus and noticed a taxi outside the library across the street. It took me a moment before I realized that Holly was in the taxi. She got out and ran up the stairs to the library. Holly and libraries were something that I did not usually **connect** in my mind. I was now very interested, so I followed her inside the library and sat a few tables away from her. She was wearing her dark glasses and had many books on her table. She read them quickly, from one book to the next. She had a pencil and was writing as she read. After a while, she put on her **lipstick** and left.

After she left, I walked over to her table and saw that they were books about Brazil.

On Christmas Eve, Holly and Mag had a party.

"Look in the bedroom," Holly said when I arrived. "There's a present for you."

I went into the bedroom and saw the beautiful birdcage on her bed.

"But, Holly! You think that it's horrible!" I said.

"I know, but I thought you wanted it?" she replied, walking into the room.

"I do! But it's so expensive. It's $350!"

I started to kiss her, but she stopped me and said, "Just promise me you will never put a living thing inside it."

"I have something for you, too," I said. "I'm afraid it's nothing much." It was true. The present was a St. Christopher medal and looked a lot smaller next to the large birdcage. But it was from Tiffany's.

"It brings good luck to travelers," I said.

"Give it to me," she said, holding her hand out.

Holly was not a girl who could keep anything. I'm sure that she has now lost that medal and left it in a suitcase or some hotel bedroom. But the birdcage is still mine, and I have taken it all over the world. I often forget that it was Holly who gave it to me because I choose to forget.

Not long after Christmas, sometime in February, we had an argument. Holly went on a winter vacation with Rusty, Mag, and José. When she returned, she was brown, and her hair was light from the sun. She seemed happy.

"At first we were in Florida," she said. "Rusty got angry at some sailors, or the sailors were angry at him. Anyway, he had to go to the hospital, and then Mag had to go to the hospital, too, because she was burned from the sun. It looked horrible. José and I left them in the hospital and went to Cuba. Rusty thinks that I would love Brazil, but I really loved Cuba. When we got back to Florida, Mag was sure that I was sleeping with José. So was Rusty. It was quite worrying until Mag and I had a talk."

We were in the living room. It was nearly March, but the Christmas tree was still sitting in the corner. There was also a new bed in the living room, which Holly was lying on under a sun lamp. She was trying to keep her skin brown.

"Does she know that you weren't sleeping with José?" I asked.

"'Of course I'm not sleeping with him. I'm a lesbian,' I told her."

"There is no way she believed that," I said, surprised.

"She did. Why do you think she bought this bed? She won't sleep in the same bed as me any more. Can you put some **oil** on my back, please?" she said.

I put some oil on her back and moved it around with my hands.

"O. J. Berman's in New York," she said. "I gave him your story, the one that was published. He liked it. He thinks he could help you, but he says that you might be writing about the wrong things. Black people and children? Who cares?"

"Not Mr. Berman, it seems," I said.

"I agree with him. I read the story twice. It doesn't mean anything."

My hands were still on her back, and I was starting to get angry.

"Give me an example of something that means something to you then," I said.

"*Wuthering Heights*," she said, immediately. "I cried so many times when I watched it."

"Oh," I said, "the *movie* not the book."

I could feel her body harden.

"Everybody has to feel important to somebody," she said. "But maybe you should try and write something that means something before you think that you are better than everybody else."

"I don't think that I am better than you or Berman. We just want different things," I said.

"Don't you want to make money?" she said.

"I haven't planned that far yet," I replied.

"That's how your stories read," she said. "Like you have written them without knowing the end. You need to make money. You have an expensive mind. Not many people are going to buy you birdcages."

"Sorry," I said. My hands were pushing into her back.

"You will be sorry if you hit me. You wanted to a minute ago, I could feel it in your hand, and you want to hit me now."

It was true. I *did* want to hit her.

"Oh no, I'm not sorry," I said. "I'm only sorry that you used your money on me. I'm sure it's difficult making money from Rusty Trawler all the time."

Holly sat up. The sun lamp was on her face, and I could see that she was angry.

"It should take you about four seconds to walk from here to the door," she said. "I'll give you two."

I left quickly and ran upstairs to my apartment. I picked up the birdcage, ran back downstairs and left it outside her front door. That finished that. Or so I thought, until the next morning when I was leaving for work. I saw the cage outside the brownstone on the side of the street. I felt a little **embarrassed**, so I picked it up and carried it back to my apartment. I was still angry with Holly. She was, I decided, a phony, and someone who I never wanted to speak to again.

CHAPTER SEVEN
A strange man

Holly and I did not talk for a while. When I saw her on the stairs, I turned my head. When I saw her in Joe Bell's bar, I walked out. Madame Sapphia Spanella, who lived on the first floor, was also angry at Holly. She did not like the late-night parties and all the men in Holly's apartment. She wanted Holly to leave the brownstone.

As April changed to May, the nights became warmer, and Holly's apartment became louder. It was never surprising to see men outside of Holly's apartment, but late that spring I saw a strange man looking at her mailbox. He looked about 50 years old and had tired eyes. He was wearing an old and dirty gray hat and a cheap blue summer suit. He never rang the doorbell but kept moving his fingers across her name.

That evening, on my way to dinner, I saw the man again. He was standing across the street next to a tree and staring at Holly's window. I began to worry. Was he a police officer? Or someone in the mafia, like her friend Sally Tomato? I suddenly felt my feelings for Holly come back, so I decided to tell Holly about the man after dinner. As I walked to the corner, I could feel the man watching me. Without turning my head, I knew that he was walking behind me because I could hear him singing. It was the same song that Holly sometimes played on her guitar.

"Excuse me," I said, turning round. "What do you want?"

The question did not seem to **embarrass** him, and he seemed happy to answer it.

"I need a friend," he said.

He pulled out a photograph. It was a picture of seven people in front of a house that was made of wood. Six of them were children, and the other person was him.

"That's me," he said, pointing at himself. "That's her," he said, pointing to one of the children. "And this one is her brother, Fred."

I looked at "her" again and, yes, that small, fat child *was* Holly. At that same moment, I suddenly realized who the man was.

"You're Holly's father."

The man seemed confused. "Her name's not Holly," he said. "She's called Lulamae Barnes. Well, she was until she married me. I am her husband, Doc Golightly. I'm a horse doctor and a farmer. I live in Texas." The man paused. "Why are you smiling?"

"I'm not," I said. "I'm just surprised."

"This is not funny. I've spent four years looking for her. As soon as I got a letter from Fred that told me where she was, I bought a ticket to come here. Lulamae belongs at home with her husband and her children."

"Her children?" I said, again surprised.

"Yes," he said, pointing to the photograph. "They are her children."

"But Holly can't be the mother of those children. They look older and bigger than she is," I said, looking at the photograph.

"OK, they are not *her* children, but they need her. Their real mother died in 1936. I married Lulamae after that, but then she ran away."

He waited for me to say something, but I did not have anything to say.

"Do you believe me?" he said, finally.

I did believe him. O. J. Berman also said the same thing at Holly's party, *Nobody knows where she comes from.*

"She broke our hearts when she ran away," the horse doctor **repeated**. "I don't know why she ran away. All the housework was done by her daughters. Lulamae had nothing to do. She just ate and got fat while her brother grew and grew. She and Fred weren't always like that. It was my oldest daughter, Nellie, who first found them. 'Papa, there are two children in the kitchen. I caught them stealing milk and eggs,' she said. That was Lulamae and Fred. They were so thin and small. Their parents were dead, and they had to live with some horrible people. I can understand why she ran away from them, but I don't know why she left my house. It was her home."

He closed his eyes and put his hands on his chest.

"She was so intelligent. I showed her how to play the guitar. I cried when I asked her to marry me. She was fourteen years old, and she said, 'Why are you crying, Doc? Of course I will marry you. I've never been married before!'" Then, he laughed and opened his eyes. "Don't tell me that woman wasn't happy! We all loved her. All she did was eat, brush her hair, and look at pictures in the newspapers. She had so many newspapers."

"But what about her brother? Did he leave with her?" I said.

"No," Doc said, "Fred stayed with us until he left to become a soldier. He's a good boy, he's very good with horses. He didn't understand why Lulamae left him or her husband and children. She started writing to him a while ago. Then, he gave me her address."

I turned back round and looked at the brownstone.

"Listen," he said. "I need a friend. I don't want her to be frightened. But please can you be my friend and tell her that I am here?"

"You might be surprised that Holly, or Lulamae, has changed," I replied.

He did not answer.

The idea of introducing Holly to her husband was funny to me. I looked up at her window and hoped that Mag, Rusty, and José were there to watch it happen. We walked into the brownstone and Doc stayed at the bottom of the stairs. He put his jacket on.

"Do I look nice?" he said.

I walked upstairs toward Holly's apartment and knocked on the door. When she opened the door, I could see that she was alone. She was wearing her dark glasses and was on her way out.

"Well," she said, hitting me with her bag. "I need to leave, so I can't talk about our argument now. We can talk tomorrow, OK?"

"Sure, Lulamae. If you're still around tomorrow," I said.

She took off her glasses.

"He told you that?" she said, her voice shaking. "Fred! Where are you?"

She immediately ran out of her apartment shouting Fred's name. Then, she suddenly stopped when she saw Doc standing at the bottom of the stairs.

"Wow, Lulamae," he said. "You're so thin, just like when I first saw you."

Holly did not move. She did not look scared but more disappointed.

"Hello, Doc," she said, after a couple of seconds. She then walked toward him and touched his face.

"Hello, Doc," she repeated. The **disappointment** was not there any more.

Doc picked her up, and they started to laugh.

"Wow, Lulamae! I can't believe it," he shouted, holding her in his arms.

I decided to leave them alone and go up to my apartment. They did not notice me leave nor did they notice Madame Sapphia Spanella shouting, "Be quiet. Take your men somewhere else!"

The next day, around noon, Holly and I met in Joe Bell's bar.

"Two more please, Mr. Bell," she said.

Joe Bell did not look happy. This was our third drink, and he wanted us to stop.

"But it's Sunday, Mr. Bell. The clocks are slow on Sunday, and I haven't been to bed yet," Holly said. "Not to sleep anyway." Holly suddenly looked away, embarrassed, something she never did.

"Well, I had to. Doc really loves me, you know? And I love him. He might be old and tired. But you don't know how sweet he is. He has really helped me, and I owe him a lot. Please don't laugh," she said.

"I'm not laughing. I'm smiling. You're the most amazing person."

"Yes, I am," she said.

"So, what else did you do last night?" I asked.

"We spent the rest of the night at the bus station. He wanted me to come home with him, but I kept telling him that I wasn't Lulamae any more. But the worst part, and I realized it when I was standing there, was that I *am* Lulamae. I'm still stealing eggs and running away. Only now, I call it having the mean reds."

"You should get a **divorce**," I said.

"Get a divorce?" she said. "I was only fourteen. It wasn't *real.*"

Joe Bell came back with our drinks.

"Never love a wild thing, Mr. Bell," Holly said. "That was Doc's mistake. He was always saving things. Sometimes it was a bird with a hurt wing or an animal with a broken leg. But you can't give your heart to a wild thing because the more you do, the stronger they get. Then, they are strong enough to run away or fly into the sky. That is what happens when you love a wild thing, Mr. Bell."

"No more drinks for you," Joe Bell said.

"Doc knew what I meant," Holly continued. "I explained it to him very carefully, and it was something that he could understand. We said goodbye and hugged, and he said he hoped that I was happy."

"What is she talking about?" Joe Bell asked me.

Holly picked up her drink. "I hope that Doc is happy, too," she said.

She touched her glass against mine. "To Doc," she said.

CHAPTER EIGHT
A different Holly

RUSTY TRAWLER MARRIES FOURTH WIFE. I was on a train somewhere in Brooklyn when I saw it written on a newspaper. The newspaper belonged to another person on the train. It was the only thing I could read, not that I wanted to read any more. Holly married him. I wanted to fall under the wheels of the train. How could she marry that stupid child, Rusty Trawler?

I was not happy during that time. I lost my job, and I could not find another one. This is what I was doing on the train. I was looking for a new job, and it was going very badly. This and the hot New York summer made me feel even worse. Now I had the mean reds, too.

When I arrived at my station, I bought a newspaper and read the rest of the story. *Millionaire Rutherfurd "Rusty" Trawler married the beautiful Miss Margaret Thatcher Fitzhue Wildwood.* Mag! I was happy that it was Mag and not Holly. I also realized that I was in love with Holly myself.

When I arrived back at the brownstone, Madame Sapphia Spanella met me in the hall. Her eyes were wide, and she was waving her hands.

"Run," she said. "Call the police. She is killing somebody! Somebody is killing her!"

It sounded like a huge animal was running around in Holly's apartment.

"Run!" Madame Spanella screamed again. "Tell the police."

I ran upstairs to Holly's door and knocked loudly. The noise stopped, but she did not answer the door. I tried to kick the door open, but it only hurt my leg. I could hear Madame Spanella shouting at another man to call the police.

"Shut up," the man's voice said. "Move out of my way."

I quickly realized that the man was José Ybarra-Jaegar. He did not look as intelligent nor as handsome as he usually did. He looked worried and scared.

"Move," he said, this time to me.

He took a key and opened the door. "She is in here, Dr. Goldman."

Another man appeared behind him and walked into the apartment. I followed them into the room. There were eggs on the walls and the cat without a name was drinking milk from the floor. The lamp was broken, and I stepped on Holly's glasses, which were lying on the floor. I looked toward her bedroom and saw Holly on her bed.

"You're a very tired young girl. You want to go to sleep, don't you?" the doctor was saying, taking her arm.

Holly touched her face and started to cry.

"He's the only one who would let me hug him on cold nights. I saw a place in Mexico with horses by the sea," she said.

The doctor took a **needle** from his bag and put it in Holly's arm.

"Didn't hurt a bit, did it?" he said, putting the needle back into his bag.

"Is it because of what happened?" José asked.

"Everything hurts. Where are my glasses?" Holly said. But she did not need them. Her eyes were closing, and she went to sleep.

"Is it because of what happened?" José asked again, angry that he had to repeat himself.

"Please, sir," the doctor said. "You need to leave."

José left the room and immediately shouted at Madame Spanella, who was standing at the door.

"Don't touch me! I'll call the police," she said as José pushed her out of the apartment.

He turned round and looked at me. I thought that he wanted me to leave, too, but surprisingly he asked me to stay and have a drink.

"I am worried," he said in his strong Brazilian accent. "I'm worried there will be a **scandal** with her breaking everything and shouting like this. It is difficult. My name and work are too important. I know her heart is broken, but first she was sad, then she broke the lamp. Now, I am scared."

"But why?" I asked. "Why is she sad about Rusty? She should be happy that he married Mag and not her. I would be."

"Rusty?" José said. He looked confused.

I was still carrying my newspaper. I showed him the page.

"Oh, that," he said, smiling. "They thought that they were breaking our hearts, but we do not care. We are happy. We laugh about it. No, it's this."

His eyes looked for something on the floor. Then, he picked up a ball of yellow paper and gave it to me. It was a letter from Doc. Holly's brother, Fred, was dead.

Holly never talked about her brother again. She also stopped calling me Fred. June, July, and all through the warm months, she stayed inside like an animal in the winter. Her hair turned darker, and she stopped caring about her clothes. José moved into her apartment and Mag Wildwood's name on the mailbox changed to *José Ybarra-Jaegar.* Holly was still alone most of the time because José was in Washington three days a week. While he was gone, Holly stayed inside, only leaving on Thursdays to visit Sally Tomato.

It might sound sad, but it was not. Holly seemed to be much happier than before. She seemed to enjoy staying at home and looking after José. She bought some chairs and tables for the apartment and learned how to cook.

"José says that I'm a great cook, can you believe it? A month ago, I couldn't even make eggs," she told me.

But she still could not cook. Even easy things like meat and salad were difficult for her. She fed José, and sometimes me, things like chicken and rice with chocolate sauce and something called tobacco cake. She was learning Portuguese, which I would listen to every time

I visited her. And she talked about her future with José, starting sentences with, "After we're married," or, "When we move to Rio."

But José did not seem interested in getting married, something that Holly knew.

"But he knows I'm having a baby, so he should ask me to marry him soon," she said, sounding hopeful. "I'm six weeks. I don't know why that should surprise you. I wasn't surprised, not one bit. I'm so happy. I want to have nine babies all with bright-green, beautiful eyes. José is a nice man, better than all the other men that I've slept with. Yes, he tells little lies, and he worries what people might think. He takes about fifty baths a day and always turns his back when he takes his clothes off. He also makes too much noise when he eats. He isn't perfect, and there are other men and women in the world who are better. A person should be able to marry a man or a woman. I'm serious. Love should be allowed with anybody. I love José. Good things only happen to you if you are good. Good? Being true to yourself is more what I mean. Anything that stops me from being a phony."

Our friendship became stronger and much closer during the end of summer. When José was in Washington, we usually spent the evenings together or went out walking. One time, we walked for five hours. We had lunch, bought some drinks, and stole some paper hats. We then walked across the Brooklyn Bridge and watched the ships move across the water.

"Years from now," she said, "one of those ships will bring me back to New York. Me and my nine Brazilian babies. They must see this, the lights, the river. I love New York. I know it isn't mine, but I know that I belong to it."

"Oh, please shut up," I said, feeling jealous. Jealous that she was going on an adventure, and I had to stay here, alone.

CHAPTER NINE
A birthday to remember

When fall arrived, so did one of the strangest days of my life. It happened on September 30th, which was also my birthday. I was downstairs waiting for the postman when I saw Holly on her way out.

"Come on," Holly said. "I'm going to walk the horses around the park. Come with me."

She was wearing a riding jacket and a pair of blue jeans and boots.

"Don't worry about this," she said, pointing to her growing stomach. "But there is a horse called Mabel Minerva, and I can't go without saying goodbye to her."

"Goodbye?" I asked, feeling confused.

"Yes, José bought tickets to Brazil. We leave next Saturday."

I was surprised and a little sad.

"We change planes in Miami," she continued. "Then over the sea and over the Andes."

"But you can't," I said. "What about, well, you can't leave everybody."

"I don't think anyone will miss me. I have no friends," she said.

"I will miss you. So will Joe Bell. And a lot of people, like Sally. Poor Mr. Tomato."

"I loved old Sally. I haven't visited him in a month.

He knows that I'm marrying José, and he was happy. I think he was worried that the police might realize that I wasn't his real niece. The fat lawyer, Mr. O'Shaughnessy, sent me $500 as a present from Sally."

"When and *if* you marry José, then I will buy you a present, too," I said. I wanted to be unkind.

"He'll marry me. Don't worry," she said, laughing. "In a nice place with his family there. That's why we are waiting until we get to Rio."

"Does he know that you're married already?" I said.

"What's the matter with you? It's a beautiful day. Why are you being horrible?" she said, angrily. "If you tell anybody, I'll kill you. Anyway, it's not real. I was only fourteen, remember?"

We did not talk again until we arrived at the park. Holly said hello to Mabel and then chose an old but beautiful black-and-white horse for me to ride.

"Don't worry. She's safe," Holly said.

I was happy because I knew nothing about horses. Holly helped me get on my horse before getting on her own. We then rode through the park and on to a path where the yellow and red leaves were the color of Holly's hair.

"See?" she shouted from behind me. "It's great!"

And it *was* great. I loved her enough to forget myself and my disappointment that she was leaving. I was just happy that she was happy.

Suddenly, everything changed when a group of young people appeared from nowhere and started throwing things at my horse. It became scared and started running quickly through the park. I tried to hold on and could hear people shouting for me to stop. I could hear Holly riding behind me and trying to get my horse to slow down. In minutes, I was across the park and on the street, riding toward taxis and buses. A policeman on a horse appeared next to me. Holly was now on the other side of me. All three horses were galloping through the streets of New York City like we were in a race.

Finally, the policeman and Holly stopped my horse. It was then, at last, that I fell off of its back and on to the road. I stood up, not sure where I was. The policeman got off of his horse and angrily wrote in his book. The policeman then took the horses away while Holly put us in the back of a taxi.

"How do you feel?" Holly said. She sounded worried.

"Fine," I replied, unsure what was happening.

"But I can't feel your heartbeat," she said, touching my neck.

"Then I must be dead."

"No, you are stupid. This is serious. Look at me," she said.

The problem was that I could not see just one Holly, but four.

"It's OK. I don't feel anything. I'm just embarrassed," I said.

"Are you sure? Please don't lie. I thought you were dead."

"But I'm not. And thank you for saving my life. You are wonderful. I love you."

"Don't be stupid," she said.

Holly kissed me on the head, and I closed my eyes.

CHAPTER TEN
A new start

That evening, photographs of Holly were all over the newspapers, but it was not about the horses. The newspapers said: ACTRESS **ARRESTED** FOR HELPING MAFIA WITH **DRUG SMUGGLING** (*Daily News*), DRUG **ARREST** FOR GIRL GOLIGHTLY (*Daily Mirror*).

There was one picture of Holly entering the police station. She was standing between two police officers and still wearing her riding clothes. She also had on her dark glasses and was smoking a Picayune cigarette. Under the photograph, it said, *Miss Golightly, the ex-girlfriend of millionaire Rutherfurd Trawler, was arrested at her expensive apartment in Manhattan. She was caught pretending to be the niece of the drug* ***smuggler*** *Salvatore "Sally" Tomato. Mr. Tomato, who was born in Cefalù, Sicily, in 1874, was sent to prison for drug smuggling. His lawyer, Oliver O'Shaughnessy, has stayed silent, but Miss Golightly was not so quiet. "Don't ask me, because I do not know," she told the newspapers. "Yes, I have visited Sally Tomato. I saw him every Thursday. What's wrong with that? No, Mr. Tomato never talked about drugs to me. He is a friendly person and a very nice old man."*

The one large mistake in the report was that she was not arrested in her "expensive apartment," but in my own bathroom. I was lying in the bath after my horse-riding accident and Holly, a helpful nurse, was sitting on the side of the bath. There was a knock at the front door. In came Madame Sapphia Spanella with two police officers. One of them was a woman and the other was a man.

"Here she is, the wanted woman!" Madame Spanella shouted as she walked into the bathroom.

She pointed a finger at Holly. The policeman seemed embarrassed because I was **naked**. The policewoman seemed to enjoy it and walked toward Holly.

"Come on. You're going to prison," the policewoman said, taking Holly's arm.

"Get your dirty hands off me, you old cow," Holly shouted.

The policewoman hit Holly hard in the face and pulled her out of the bathroom with the help of the policeman. I jumped out of the bath and followed them as far as the front door. I was still naked.

"Don't forget!" Holly shouted as she was pulled down the stairs. "Please feed the cat."

I did not realize how bad Holly's arrest was until that evening when Joe Bell came to my apartment and showed me the newspapers.

"Do you think it's true?" he asked me. "Did she visit Sally Tomato in prison?"

"Well, yes," I said. He did not seem happy with my reply.

"I thought you were her friend!" he shouted.

"Wait a minute. I didn't say that she knew what she was doing. But, yes, she did send messages."

"She could get ten years in prison for helping to **smuggle** drugs," he said. "You know her friends. The rich ones. Come to the bar, and we can phone them. She is going to need their help."

When we arrived at the bar, Joe made me a drink and gave me the telephone, but I did not know who to phone. José was in Washington, and I did not know how to reach him. I did not know any of her other friends. Maybe Holly was right. Maybe she didn't have any friends. I decided to try Rusty Trawler, so I rang the **operator** and asked for his number. It was Mag Wildwood who answered the phone.

"Are you stupid?" Mag said when I asked for her help. "If anyone connects our names with that h-h-horrible girl, we will call our lawyers. I always knew she was bad. Prison is where she belongs, and my husband agrees with me."

I put down the telephone and thought about ringing Doc Golightly. No, Holly might be angry, I thought. I rang the operator again and asked for O. J. Berman's number.

"Is this about Holly?" he said when I explained who I was. "I know already. I've spoken to the best lawyer in New York. I asked him to help Holly and to send me the bill, but I told him not to connect my name with her. I told you what she was like. She's a phony, but a *real* phony, you know? Anyway, don't worry. She will be home tonight."

But she did not come home that night, or the next morning. I had no key to her apartment, so I used the fire escape to get inside and feed her cat. I found the cat in the bedroom and quickly realized that he was not alone. There was a man in the bedroom, too, and he was putting clothes into a suitcase. I looked at him while he looked at me. His face was handsome, and he looked like José. The suitcase also had José's clothes inside.

"Did Mr. Ybarra-Jaegar send you?" I asked.

"I am his cousin," he said, in the same Brazilian accent as José.

"He can't leave her," I said.

The cousin laughed and continued putting José's clothes into the suitcase. When he finished, he stood up and gave me a letter.

"This is from my cousin. Can you give it to her?" he said.

"Where is José?" I said, but the man only repeated his question.

I sat down on Holly's bed and pulled her cat close to me. I felt as badly for Holly as she could feel for herself.

"Yes, I will," I replied, finally.

And I did, but I did not want to. It was two mornings later, and I was sitting with Holly in the hospital. She was taken there on the night of her arrest.

"Well, darling," she said when I arrived. "I lost the baby."

I gave her a pack of Picayune cigarettes and some cheap flowers. She was not wearing her dark glasses, and her eyes were like rainwater. I was surprised at how ill she looked.

"I couldn't tell you about the fat woman since I

didn't know about her myself until my brother died. I didn't know what it meant, Fred dying, and then I saw her. She was there in the room with me, and she had Fred in her arms. A fat, mean, red woman in a chair. She was laughing so loudly. Now, do you understand why I broke everything in my apartment?"

Then, she asked about José. The moment she saw the letter she closed her eyes.

"Darling," she said. "Can you get my lipstick from my bag? A girl cannot read something like this without her lipstick."

She took out a mirror and put on some lipstick. She then put on a pearl necklace. She opened the letter and began to read. When she finished reading, she asked for a Picayune.

"Maybe one day you can write about this," she said, throwing me the letter. "Can you read it? I want to hear it myself."

I began, "My dearest little girl."

Holly at once interrupted. She wanted to know what I thought of the handwriting. I thought nothing.

"Go on," she said.

"My dearest little girl. I have loved you knowing that you were not like normal people. But, after your arrest, I can see that you are very different from the wife that I wanted. I have my family, my job, and my name to think about. I'm sorry. I'm too scared. Forget me, beautiful child. I have gone home."

"In a way, it's quite nice," she said.

"Nice!" I said, feeling surprised. "How is it nice?"

"He says that he is scared, and I can understand that."

I knew Holly was lying because she suddenly started to cry.

"I loved him," she said, taking another cigarette.

"Thank you for being such a terrible horse rider. That's why I'm in the hospital and not in prison. The police think that it was because that policewoman hit me and not because of the horse."

"What are you going to do?" I said. "We have to make plans."

"Why do you care?" Holly replied.

"You're my friend, and I'm worried. I want to know what you are going to do about this."

"Today is Wednesday, isn't it?" she asked. "I will sleep until Saturday, and then, in the morning, I will go to the bank. Then, as you already know, I still have a plane ticket to Brazil. And, since you are such a good friend, you can wave me goodbye. Please stop shaking your head."

"Holly. Holly. You can't do that."

"I'm not going because of José, if that is what you think? I still have the ticket that he paid for and I've never been to Brazil."

"You have been arrested. If they catch you, they will send you to prison. And, if you go to Brazil, you will never be able to come home," I said.

"I don't care. Anyway, home is where you feel at home. I'm still looking."

"No, Holly. You need to stay."

"Don't worry, darling," she said, still smoking her cigarette. "I can't stay here. Nobody will talk to me now that I was arrested. My name will always mean scandal, and Sally Tomato won't allow me to talk to the police anyway. But there is *something* that you can do for me."

"What?" I replied.

"Find the names of the fifty richest men in Brazil, and then go to my apartment and find that St. Christopher medal you gave me. I'll need it for my journey."

CHAPTER ELEVEN

Holly's final day

On Saturday, the day Holly was leaving, there was a storm. I did not think that the plane would fly, but Holly was sure and continued with her plans. I went to her apartment to get the St. Christopher medal. She also asked me to get her guitar, toothbrush, and the cat, then meet her at Joe Bell's bar.

It was difficult going up and down the fire escape in the strong wind and heavy rain. I did not know how to carry the cat, so I put him inside an empty **pillowcase**, which he did not like. The bar was not far from the apartment, but the guitar filled up with rain, the toothbrush fell on the floor, and the cat screamed. But, worse, I was scared, just like José. I was scared the police were going to arrest me for helping her.

"You're late," Holly said as I entered the bar. "Did you bring the cat?"

The cat jumped out of the pillowcase and into Holly's arms.

"Mr. Bell, three drinks, please."

"You'll need only two," he said, standing next to a bowl of his flowers. "I won't drink to this."

Joe was angry that Holly was leaving, and the more she spoke about going to Brazil, the angrier he became. Suddenly, a large black car appeared outside the bar. Holly, the first to notice it, quickly looked behind her, thinking that it was the police. So did I until I saw Joe Bell look away. He was embarrassed.

"It's nothing. I rented it to take you to the airport," Joe said.

"Kind, dear Mr. Bell. Look at me, please," Holly said.

He turned round and took the flowers from the bowl. He tried to throw them to her, but he missed, and the flowers fell on the floor.

"Goodbye," he said, his face turning red. He ran to the bathroom and shut the door.

The driver of the black car was quiet and did not seem to care when Holly took off her riding clothes and changed into a small black dress. We did not talk as talk usually turned into an argument. Holly also seemed interested in something else and was looking out the window.

"Stop here," she said to the driver.

We were in the middle of a dangerous area. There was trash on the street, which was made worse by the heavy rain and wind. Holly stepped out of the car, taking the cat with her.

"What do you think?" she said, hugging him. "This should be the right kind of place for a strong cat like you. There is a lot of trash, and other cats to make friends with."

She put him on the floor, but, when he did not move, she started to shout.

"Go!" she said, loudly. But the cat stayed next to her.

"Go!" she shouted again. "I said go!"

Holly jumped back into the car and shut the door.

"Go," she told the driver.

"I can't believe you did that," I said, feeling surprised. "Why did you do that?"

"We never made any promises. We just met next to the river, that's all," she said, but her voice broke, and her face was white.

The car stopped at a traffic light. Suddenly, Holly opened the door once again and jumped out. She ran down the street, and this time I ran after her. But the cat was not there.

"Cat. Where are you?" she shouted. "Here, cat!"

I took Holly's arm and tried to walk her back to the car.

"Oh no, we *did* belong to each other. He was mine," she said, starting to cry.

"I'll find him," I said. "I will come back and find him, I promise."

Holly smiled. "But what about me?" she said. "I'm scared. Not knowing what's yours until you've thrown it away. The mean reds, they're nothing. The fat woman, she is nothing. This is much worse."

She stepped into the car and fell into the seat. "Sorry, driver, we can go," she said.

CHAPTER TWELVE
A letter

GOLIGHTLY GIRL GONE. And: DRUG SCANDAL ACTRESS CONNECTED TO MAFIA. Then, sometime later: GOLIGHTLY GIRL SEEN IN RIO. She was on the front page of every newspaper.

The police did not try to find Holly, and her name only appeared in the newspaper one more time, on Christmas Day, when Sally Tomato died in Sing Sing prison. After that, there was nothing. One month turned into many winter months, and I did not hear from Holly. A man called Quaintance Smith moved into her apartment. Like Holly, he also had many men in his apartment. But Madame Spanella seemed to love the young man and did not care about his loud parties.

In the spring, a letter came. It was written in pencil and signed with a lipstick kiss.

Brazil was horrible but Buenos Aires is the best. Not Tiffany's, but almost. I've met a ($$) man. Love? I think so. I'm looking for somewhere to live ($$ has a wife and seven children). I will send you my address when I know it myself.

But she did not send the address. I was disappointed as there was so much that I wanted to tell her. I was making money from my writing, Rusty and Mag were **divorced**, and I was moving out of the brownstone. But, mostly, I wanted to tell her about her cat. I kept my promise and went looking for him every day. Then, one cold Sunday afternoon, I saw him. He was lying in the window of a warm-looking house. He looked happy, and he looked like he had a name and was somewhere that he belonged. In an African village or somewhere else, I hope Holly is, too.

During-reading questions

CHAPTER ONE

1 Why do the writer and Holly go to Joe Bell's bar six or seven times a week?

CHAPTER TWO

1 Why does Holly ask if she can call the writer Fred?
2 Where does Holly go on Thursdays?

CHAPTER THREE

1 Why does the writer write Holly a note telling her that tomorrow is Thursday?
2 Why does Holly want O. J. Berman to help the writer?

CHAPTER FOUR

1 What does Holly mean when she says that she was "using" O. J. Berman?
2 What are the mean reds?

CHAPTER FIVE

1 Why is the writer confused about Mag still being in Holly's apartment?

CHAPTER SIX

1 Why does Holly not like the zoo or the birdcage?
2 Why do the writer and Holly have an argument?

CHAPTER SEVEN

1 How does Doc Golightly find out where Holly lives?

CHAPTER EIGHT

1 Who does Rusty Trawler marry?
2 Why is Holly sad?

CHAPTER NINE

1 When is Holly leaving for Brazil?

CHAPTER TEN

1 Where are the writer and Holly when Holly is arrested?
2 Why do Mag Wildwood and O. J. Berman not want their names connected with Holly?

CHAPTER ELEVEN

1 Why does Holly leave her cat on the street?

CHAPTER TWELVE

1 Why does Madame Sapphia Spanella like Quaintance Smith and not Holly, do you think?
2 Will the writer ever see Holly again, do you think?

After-reading questions

1 How does Holly change during the book?
2 Is Holly is a good person or a bad person, do you think? Why?
3 Does the writer love Holly, do you think? Why/Why not?
4 The writer never tells us his name. Why is this, do you think?
5 Why is the book called *Breakfast at Tiffany's*, do you think?

Exercises

CHAPTER ONE

1 Write the correct question word. Then, answer the questions in your notebook.

When What Where Who Who

1 ...*When*... does the writer live in the brownstone?
He lives there in the early 1940s.
2 .... lives in the apartment below?
3 .... is Joe Bell's bar?
4 .... goes skating in Central Park every afternoon?
5 .... does Holly always lose?

CHAPTERS TWO AND THREE

2 Write the correct verb form, *past simple* or *past continuous*, in your notebook.

1 My heart ***was moving*** / **moved** so fast from the surprise of seeing Holly on my fire escape that it **was taking / took** me a moment to say anything.
2 I **was making / made** her a drink and **was sitting / sat** in the chair opposite her.
3 When I **finished / was finishing** reading, I could see that Holly was bored.
4 I **looked / was looking** round at her face and **was seeing / saw** that her eyes **were / was** wet.
5 The next day, I **came / was coming** home and **found / was finding** a message from Holly in my mailbox.
6 I **was wanting / wanted** her to be an actress, so I helped her change her accent, and I **taught / was teaching** her some French.

CHAPTER FOUR

3 Complete these sentences in your notebook, using the names from the box.

The writer	Holly Golightly	O. J. Berman	Rusty Trawler

1 ......*The writer*...... is standing alone at the party.
2 .... has three ex-wives.
3 .... is able to help the writer.
4 .... goes to Tiffany's when she is sad.

CHAPTER FIVE

4 Make these sentences negative in your notebook.

1 The next day, I saw Holly on the stairs.
The next day, I didn't see Holly on the stairs...............................
2 He had brown hair and was wearing a nice suit.
3 "But he does laugh," she said.
4 "Yes," Holly said, lying down. "Maybe I should."

CHAPTER SIX

5 Match the phrasal verbs with their definitions in your notebook.

Example: *1—b*

1	look for (something)	a	to move something you wear on to your body
2	put (something) on	b	to try to find someone or something
3	try on (something)	c	to hold or move someone or something
4	pick (something) up	d	to wear clothes to see how they look and check the size

CHAPTER SEVEN

6 Are these sentences *true* or *false*? Write the correct answers in your notebook.

1 Madame Sapphia Spanella wants Holly to stay in the brownstone. ....*false*............
2 The man is singing the same song that Holly sometimes plays on her guitar.
3 There are eight people in the photograph.
4 Holly's real name is Lulamae Barnes.
5 The children in the photograph are not Holly's children.
6 Holly is frightened when she sees Doc.
7 The writer meets Holly in Joe Bell's bar two days later.
8 Holly is awake all night.

CHAPTER EIGHT

7 Correct these sentences in your notebook.

1 RUSTY TRAWLER MARRIES FIFTH WIFE.
RUSTY TRAWLER MARRIES FOURTH WIFE............
2 I looked toward her bathroom and saw Holly on the floor.
3 It was a letter from Fred. Holly's brother, Doc, was dead.
4 While he was gone, Holly stayed inside, only leaving on Mondays to visit Sally Tomato.
5 She was learning French, which I would listen to every time I visited her.
6 A person shouldn't be able to marry a man or a woman
7 We then ran across the Brooklyn Bridge and watched the ships move across the water.
8 "Oh, please shut up," I said, feeling angry. Angry that she was going on an adventure, and I had to stay here, alone.

CHAPTER NINE

8 Complete these sentences in your notebook, using the words from the box.

nothing	path	behind	hold on	race	nowhere	slow down

I was happy because I knew [1]........*nothing*........ about horses. Holly helped me get on my horse before getting on her own. We then rode through the park and on to a [2].......... where the yellow and red leaves were the color of Holly's hair. "See?" she shouted from [3].......... me. "It's great!" And it *was* great. I loved her enough to forget myself and my disappointment that she was leaving. I was just happy that she was happy. Suddenly, everything changed when a group of young people appeared from [4].......... and started throwing things at my horse. It became scared and started running quickly through the park. I tried to [5].......... and could hear people shouting for me to stop. I could hear Holly riding behind me and trying to get my horse to [6].......... In minutes, I was across the park and on the street, riding toward taxis and buses. A policeman on a horse appeared next to me. Holly was now on the other side of me. All three horses were galloping through the streets of New York City like we were in a [7]..........

CHAPTER TEN

9 Match the two parts of these sentences in your notebook.

Example: *1—d*

1	There was a picture of	**a**	and some cheap flowers.
2	I jumped out of the bath	**b**	she closed her eyes.
3	I decided to try Rusty Trawler,	**c**	and followed them as far as the front door.
4	I gave her a pack of Picayune cigarettes	**d**	Holly entering the police station.
5	The moment she saw the letter	**e**	and put on some lipstick.
6	She took out a mirror	**f**	because she suddenly started to cry.
7	I knew Holly was lying	**g**	so I rang the operator and asked for his number.

CHAPTER ELEVEN

10 Who said this? Who did they say it to? Write the correct names in your notebook.

		Who spoke?	**Who to?**
1	"Did you bring the cat?"	*Holly*	*The writer*
2	"I won't drink to this."		
3	"Stop here."		
4	"Go!"		
5	"I can't believe you did that."		
6	"Oh no, we *did* belong to each other. He was mine."		

CHAPTER TWELVE

11 Put these sentences in the correct order in your notebook.

a .... The writer gets a letter from Holly.

b .... Sally Tomato dies on Christmas Day.

c .... The writer finds Holly's cat.

d ....*1*..... Holly is on the front page of every newspaper.

e .... The writer hopes that Holly belongs somewhere.

f .... Quaintance Smith moves into Holly's apartment.

Project work

1 Imagine you are one of the following characters, and write a diary page:
- Holly, after she meets the writer for the first time in his apartment
- Mag Wildwood, the day after the party
- José, on the day Holly finds out that her brother has died.

2 Write a newspaper report about one of these things:
- Rusty Trawler and Holly Golightly are going to get married
- The writer's horse racing through New York City
- GOLIGHTLY GIRL SEEN IN RIO.

3 Compare the book to the movie. How are they the same/different? Why were these changes made, do you think?

4 What do you think happens to Holly after the story? Write another chapter by the writer or Holly, five years in the future.

5 Write about the life of women in North America/your country now. How have things changed since the 1940s?

An answer key for all questions and exercises can be found at **www.penguinreaders.co.uk**

Glossary

accent (n.)
a way of saying words that shows the place or country that a person comes from

actress (n.)
a woman actor. Today, many women who act are called "actors".

agent (n.)
An *agent* helps actors and *actresses* to get work in movies and arranges the amount of money that they will be paid.

argument (n.)
when people talk to each other in an angry way because they do not agree

arrest (v. and n.)
If someone is *arrested*, the police stop them and take them to a police station because maybe they did a crime. *Arrest* is the noun of *arrest.*

audition (n.)
when a person acts, sings, or dances in front of a group of people and then they decide if this person will be in a play, movie, etc.

behave (v.)
How someone *behaves* is the way that they do or say things. If you want someone to *behave,* you want them to be good and do or say the right things.

belong (v.)
1) to feel happy and comfortable in a place.
2) If something *belongs* to you, you own it.

carving (n.)
A *carving* is made by cutting a piece of wood, stone, etc.

childhood (n.)
the time in your life when you are a child

clown (n.)
A *clown's* job is to make people laugh by wearing funny clothes, having a painted face, and doing funny things.

confused (adj.); **confusing** (adj.)
When you are *confused*, you do not understand what is happening. When something is *confusing*, it is difficult to understand.

connect (v.)
to see or show that there is a relationship between things, ideas, or people

diamond (n.)
a beautiful, hard, clear stone used in rings, etc. *Diamonds* are very expensive.

disappointed (adj. and v.); **disappointment** (n.)
If you are *disappointed* or if something *disappoints* you, you are unhappy because something that you wanted did not happen or was not good. *Disappointment* is the noun of *disappointed.*

divorce (n. and adj.)
when people who are married decide not to be together any more.

drug (n.)
something that people take to make themselves feel happy, excited, etc. Buying and selling some *drugs* is against the law.

embarrassing (adj.); **embarrassed** (adj.); **embarrass** (v.)
If you are *embarrassed,* you feel worried about what other people think of something you did or said. If something is *embarrassing* or *embarrasses* you, it makes you feel *embarrassed.*

ex (n.)
Your *ex-wife* or *ex-girlfriend* is a woman who was your wife or girlfriend but is not any more. Your *ex-husband* or *ex-boyfriend* is a man who was your husband or boyfriend but is not any more.

hug (v.)
to put your arms round a person or animal because you love them or like them a lot

independent (adj.); **independence** (n.)
An *independent* person does not want or need other people to help them or do things for them. *Independence* is the noun of *independent.*

lesbian (n.)
a woman who wants to have sex with other women

lipstick (n.)
color that you put on your lips (= the two parts at the front of your mouth that you use to kiss someone)

mafia (n.)
a large group of criminals (= people who do crimes) who work together in the United States, Italy, and other countries

naked (adj.)
not wearing clothes

needle (n.)
a very thin piece of metal that is used to put medicine into a person's body

oil (n.)
something that you put on your skin to look after it and make it soft

operator (n.)
In the past, an *operator* worked for a telephone company and helped people make calls.

owe (v.)
to feel that you should do something for someone because they have done something for you

phony (n.)
Phony means not real. If someone is a *phony*, they are *pretending* to be someone that they are not.

pillow (n.); **pillowcase** (n.)
A *pillow* is a soft thing that you put your head on when you are in bed. A *pillowcase* is a thin piece of material that you put around a *pillow* and then it stays clean.

president (n.)
the most important person in the government (= a group of important people. They say what must happen in a country) of some countries

pretend (v.)
to make people think that something is true when it is not

publish (v.)
to put a story or information in a place where people can read it, for example in books or newspapers

realize (v.)
to know or understand something suddenly

repeat (v.)
to say or do something again

scandal (n.)
something that a lot of people talk about because they think it is wrong or bad

serious (adj.)
Someone is *serious* when they really mean what they say. Something that is *serious* is important.

smuggling (n.); **smuggler** (n.); **smuggle** (v.)
Smuggling is taking something, for example *drugs*, out of a place in a secret way. It is against the law. A *smuggler* is a person who does this. *Smuggle* is the verb of *smuggling*.

stutter (n.)
when someone *repeats* the first sound of a word when they talk, usually because they have a problem with speaking

trash (n.)
things that you do not want, like old food, paper, cans, etc.

yawn (v. and n.)
to open your mouth wide and take air in and out because you are tired or bored. *Yawn* is the noun of *yawn*.